THiS BOOK BELONGS TO:

_____

To Andrea, Lauren, and Kirsten
for helping bring these
Tiny Habitats to life

A TiNY HABiTaTS BOOK

poo pile
on the prairie

Amy Hevron

Beach Lane Books • New York London Toronto Sydney New Delhi

Behold! The majestic bison of the Great Plains!

Hear them thunder across the prairie!

Watch them mow down miles of meadows!

See them . . . poo.

Dung beetles were the first to sniff out the steamy poo pile.

Tunnelers burrowed underneath it.

Dwellers dug inside it.

Rollers carted away poo balls and buried them.

Soon, flies dropped in and laid their eggs—

thousands and thousands of eggs.

Plop!

Plop!

Plop!

Meanwhile, the poo pile sprouted with prairie violets that soaked up the sun.

As weeks flew by,
the poo pile became abuzz with life.

summer

month 4

Beetles tended to their broods.

What cutie-pies!

Little larvae became little flies—

thousands and thousands of flies.

Soon, crickets came for supper.

Sparrows nested nearby.

And burrowing owls hauled away poo balls for bait.

Meanwhile, the poo-pile garden glittered
with newly emerged butterflies.

Months of sunshine and showers transformed the poo pile into a bouquet of . . .

fragrant flowers,

graceful grasses,

Elk stopped to smell the prairie roses.

Toads stopped to smell the bug bonanza.

Grasshoppers stopped what they were doing and got out of there!

Belowground, earthworms and prairie dogs tunneled into the rich, poo-filled soil.

Meanwhile, aboveground, the poo-pile patch wilted as seeds and butterflies scattered to the wind.

As the year grew colder, the poo pile quieted, hidden under mountains of snow.

winter

month 10

Beetles snoozed inside.

Bumblebees hibernated underneath.

Baby caterpillars curled up on top.

Here's a cozy spot!

Prairie chickens burrowed for seeds and shelter.

And a fox poked around
for pocket gophers.

No thank you!

Meanwhile, as the snow melted,
the last bits of the poo pile dispersed
into the soil, becoming food for the
dormant grasses.

Behold! A baby bison bounds across the Great Plains!

spring
month 1

Hear her snort on the prairie.

Watch her munch in
fresh meadows with Mama.

See all the little life that follows in her hoof steps.

The Scoop on Bison Poop

Bison are North America's largest land animals. And where they roam, the land is littered with their poo piles. Their poo fertilizes the soil, spreads seeds, and houses and feeds hundreds of tiny grassland species. In doing so, their poo becomes an important building block for diverse prairie ecosystems.

Bison poo is high in nutrients and tiny microbes that enrich the soil. And little dung beetles play a big role in breaking it down and dispersing it across the land. Other insects, like true flies, use poo piles as nurseries. A single poo pile can house more than three hundred different species of insects during its lifetime. And this insect population boom, in turn, feeds a wide range of birds, amphibians, and small mammals, which attract bigger predators like foxes, badgers, and coyotes.

Poo piles can also contain seeds that are then spread across the prairie. Wherever bison graze, plant life is more diverse with flowers like lupines and prairie violets. These flowers are the primary food source for important native pollinators like bumblebees and rare butterflies. And this diverse foliage feeds other grazers like pronghorn deer and elk. Wildfires also play an important role in grassland life cycles. By burning piled-up dead plants and returning the nutrients to the soil in the form of ash, wildfires allow dormant plants to regrow quickly in these sunny and enriched spots. This fresh plant growth in the wake of wildfires is the favorite food for bison.

Researchers are continuing to learn more about the importance of bison and their poo in prairie ecosystems. Some great places to see North American prairie habitats are Blue Mounds State Park in Minnesota, Joseph H. Williams Tallgrass Prairie Preserve in Oklahoma, Nachusa Grasslands in Illinois, Tallgrass Prairie National Preserve in Kansas, and Yellowstone National Park in Wyoming.

Additional Reading

Bardoe, Cheryl. *Behold the Beautiful Dung Beetle.* London: Charlesbridge, 2014.

Bodden, Valerie. *Bison.* Mankato, MN: The Creative Company, 2013.

The Nature Conservancy, n.d. https://www.nature.org/en-us/get-involved/how-to-help
/places-we-protect/tallgrass-prairie-national-preserve.

Johnson, Rebecca L. *A Walk in the Prairie*, 2nd ed. Minneapolis, MN: Lerner Publications, 2021.

Selected Sources

"All About Birds." The Cornell Lab, n.d. https://www.allaboutbirds.org.

Barber, Nicholas, Sheryl C. Hosler, Peyton Whiston, and Holly P. Jones. "Initial Responses of Dung
Beetle Communities to Bison Reintroduction in Restored and Remnant Tallgrass Prairie." *Natural
Areas Journal* 39, no. 4, December 6, 2019. https://par.nsf.gov/servlets/purl/10129537.

"Bison Bellows: Grand Canyon National Park." National Park Service, April 21, 2016. https://www.nps
.gov/articles/bison-bellows-4-21-16.htm.

Hudson, Dee, and Charles Larry. "Nachusa 2023—A Year in Photos." Friends of Nachusa Grasslands,
n.d. https://www.nachusagrasslands.org/nachusa-blog.

"Last Stand of the Tallgrass Prairie." National Park Service, n.d. https://
www.nps.gov/tapr/index.htm.

Ratajczak, Zak, Scott L. Collins, John M. Blair, and Jesse B. Nippert. "*Reintroducing
Bison Results in Long-Running and Resilient Increases in Grassland Diversity.*" PNAS 119,
no. 36, August 29, 2022. https://www.pnas.org/doi/full/10.1073/pnas.2210433119.

BEACH LANE BOOKS • An imprint of Simon & Schuster Children's Publishing Division • 1230 Avenue of the Americas, New
York, New York 10020 • © 2025 by Amy Hevron • Book design by Lauren Rille • All rights reserved, including the right of
reproduction in whole or in part in any form. • BEACH LANE BOOKS and colophon are trademarks of Simon & Schuster,
LLC. • For information about special discounts for bulk purchases, please contact Simon & Schuster Special Sales at
1-866-506-1949 or business@simonandschuster.com. • The Simon & Schuster Speakers Bureau can bring authors to your
live event. For more information or to book an event, contact the Simon & Schuster Speakers Bureau at 1-866-248-3049
or visit our website at www.simonspeakers.com. • The text for this book was set in Fairplex. • The illustrations for this
book were rendered in acrylic, marker, and pencil on Bristol paper and digitally collaged. • Manufactured in China • 1024
SCP • First Edition • 10 9 8 7 6 5 4 3 2 1 • Library of Congress Cataloging-in-Publication Data • Names: Hevron, Amy,
author. • Title: Poo pile on the prairie / Amy Hevron. • Description: First edition. | New York : Beach Lane Books, [2025] |
Includes bibliographical references. | Audience: Ages 4–8 | Audience: Grades 2–3 | Summary: "This illuminating non-
fiction picture book explores the tiny habitats that emerge from bison poo piles"— Provided by publisher. • Identifiers:
LCCN 2024013229 (print) | LCCN 2024013230 (ebook) | ISBN 9781665935029 (hardcover) | ISBN 9781665935036 (ebook)
• Subjects: LCSH: Prairie ecology—Great Plains—Juvenile literature. | American bison—Ecology—Great Plains—Juvenile
literature. | Prairie animals—Great Plains—Juvenile literature. | Prairie animals—Habitat—
Great Plains—Juvenile literature. | Animal droppings—Juvenile literature. • Classification:
LCC QH104.5.G73 H48 2025 (print) | LCC QH104.5.G73 (ebook) | DDC 577.4/4097648—
dc23/eng/20240424 • LC record available at https://lccn.loc.gov/2024013229
• LC ebook record available at https://lccn.loc.gov/2024013230